THOMAS CRANE PUBLIC LIBRARY
QUINCY MA

CITY APPROPRIATION

WHY WE NEED WATER AND FIBER

By Angela Royston

Crabtree Publishing Company
www.crabtreebooks.com

Crabtree Publishing Company

www.crabtreebooks.com

Author: Angela Royston
Publishing plan research and development: Sean Charlebois, Reagan Miller
Editors: Sarah Eason, Nick Hunter, Lynn Peppas
Proofreaders: Robyn Hardyman, Kathy Middleton, Crystal Sikkens
Project coordinator: Kathy Middleton
Design: Calcium
Photo Research: Susannah Jayes
Print coordinator: Katherine Berti
Production coordinator and prepress technician: Ken Wright
Series consultant: Julie Negrin

Picture credits:
Photolibrary: Carolina Biological Supply Company 32, Dennis Kunkel 10–11
Shutterstock: cover, Austin Adams 27, Andresr 17, Galyna Andrushko 16, CandyBoxPhoto 40, Rich Carey 34–35, Christo 13, DM7 11, East 24, Fine Shine 30, Luca Grandinetti 9, Jiri Hera 39, Holbox 7, Goran Kuzmanovski 15, Mangostock 22, MC_PP 8, Monticello 20, Nattika 29, Alexandre Nunes 4, Ioannis Pantziaras 41, Pashapixel 43, Photomaru 25, Paul Prescott 19, Anatoliy Samara 33, Andrey Shadrin 31, Alex Staroseltsev 12, Konstantin Sutyagin 36, Szefei 15, Thefinalmiracle 6, Leah-Anne Thompson 23, Tihis 37, Suzanne Tucker 14, Kiselev Andrey Valerevich 21, Filipe B. Varela 10, Valentyn Volkov 18, Simone van den Berg 28, Wavebreakmedia ltd 42, XAOC 26

Library and Archives Canada Cataloguing in Publication

Royston, Angela
Why we need water and fiber / Angela Royston.

(The science of nutrition)
Includes index.
Issued also in electronic format.
ISBN 978-0-7787-1691-4 (bound).--ISBN 978-0-7787-1698-3 (pbk.)

1. Water in the body--Juvenile literature. 2. Fiber in human nutrition--Juvenile literature. I. Title.
II. Series: Science of nutrition (St. Catharines, Ont.)

QP535.H1R69 2011 j612'.01522 C2011-900213-2

Library of Congress Cataloging-in-Publication Data

Royston, Angela, 1945-
Why we need water and fiber / Angela Royston.
p. cm. -- (The science of nutrition)
Includes index.
ISBN 978-0-7787-1698-3 (pbk. : alk. paper) -- ISBN 978-0-7787-1691-4 (reinforced library binding : alk. paper) -- ISBN 978-1-4271-9682-8 (electronic (pdf))
1. Water in the body--Juvenile literature. 2. Fiber in human nutrition--Juvenile literature. I. Title. II. Series.

QP535.H1R693 2011
612'.01522--dc22

2010052766

Crabtree Publishing Company
www.crabtreebooks.com 1-800-387-7650

Printed in the U.S.A./022011/CJ20101228

Published in Canada
Crabtree Publishing
616 Welland Ave.
St. Catharines, Ontario
L2M 5V6

Published in the United States
Crabtree Publishing
PMB 59051
350 Fifth Avenue, 59th Floor
New York, New York 10118

Published in the United Kingdom
Crabtree Publishing
Maritime House
Basin Road North, Hove
BN41 1WR

Published in Australia
Crabtree Publishing
386 Mt. Alexander Rd.
Ascot Vale (Melbourne)
VIC 3032

CONTENTS

FOOD FOR FUEL

We all need to eat food and drink water to stay alive. Food contains essential nutrients your body needs to keep going and stay healthy. Different foods provide different nutrients, but some foods are healthier than others. Food also contains fiber and water, both of which are essential for good health. This book is about water and fiber.

You need nutrients

A healthy diet is one that gives you the right amount of each nutrient. The food pyramid is divided into slices. Each slice represents a group of food that is rich in a particular type of nutrient. Apart from oils and milk, each group contains foods that are also rich in fiber.

Do not forget that drinking plenty of water is an important part of a healthy diet.

The food pyramid shows healthy foods only. It does not include foods such as cookies and chips, which are high in salt, fat, or sugar.

Grains
Grains give you energy, but they also contain some protein and other nutrients.

Vegetables and fruits
You should eat a wide range from these two groups to get all the nutrients you need.

Oils and fats
These foods should not be overeaten.

Milk
This group of foods is rich in protein but can also be high in fat.

Meat and beans
These foods are rich in protein, although meats can also be high in fat.

Main nutrients

Cereal grains such as rice and wheat contain a lot of carbohydrates, which your body changes into energy. Dairy foods and oils contain fat, which also gives you energy. The meat and beans group includes foods that are packed with protein. Your body uses protein to grow and to replace damaged **cells**.

Vitamins and minerals

Vegetables and fruits contain many different vitamins and minerals. Your body needs small amounts of these nutrients to keep it working well.

WHAT ARE WATER AND FIBER?

Water and fiber are not nutrients but both are essential for basic human health. In fact, water is even more important than food. People can stay alive for about three weeks without food, but no one can survive for more than three days without water. This makes survival tough in some parts of the world, where there is very little rainfall and so little water to drink.

Body Talk

Insoluble fiber is chewier than other kinds of foods, and it is often removed from plants and discarded for that reason. For example, cartons of fruit juice contain less **insoluble fiber** than the original fruit.

Finding water is an everyday challenge in some parts of the world.

Fiber

Fiber consists of carbohydrates such as **cellulose**, which comes from the cell walls of plants and gives plants their strength. Nutrients have to be digested before the body can use them. During digestion nutrients are broken down and taken into the blood. Most fiber, however, cannot be digested and is called insoluble fiber for that reason. It passes right though your body, but it helps your body to get rid of waste called **feces**.

Soluble fiber is a carbohydrate and can be digested, although it does not give you energy like other carbohydrates. It consists mainly of **pectin**, which helps to keep your heart healthy.

Apples are a highly fibrous food. They contain pectin, an agent that helps digestion.

Try this...

Cut an orange in half and squeeze out the juice using a juicer or lemon squeezer. The solid bits left behind are mainly fiber. Oranges also contain soluble fiber, but you cannot see that. Enjoy drinking the orange juice, which is mostly water.

The water you see in springs probably fell as rain a long time ago. Some spring water may even be thousands of years old!

Did you know?

More than half of your body is water! About three-fifths of your weight is due to water.

All important water

Water is a clear liquid, which falls from the sky as rain. In many countries, water is collected in reservoirs and water tanks before it is piped to homes and other buildings. Some rainwater gathers underground, and people take it from springs or by digging wells.

You need to drink to keep your body topped up with water. Body fluids such as **saliva**, blood, and **urine** are all mainly water. Saliva in your mouth helps you to taste and to chew up food so that you can swallow it. Blood carries oxygen and nutrients to every living cell in the body, and it takes away waste. Much of the waste is converted into liquid urine.

Body Talk

Sometimes your nose runs with extra mucus. This usually happens when you have a cold or have breathed in something that irritates the lining of the nose. Mucus helps to wash **germs** and annoying particles out of your nose.

Mucus and sweat

The insides of your body are lined with watery mucus. This is the slimy stuff that coats your throat, your nose, and every surface inside your body. Sweat is salty water that oozes out of your skin. As the water dries it cools your skin, which helps keep your body cool.

Inside the cells

Most of the water in your body is in your cells. A cell consists mostly of a jelly called cytoplasm, which is mainly water.

Orange trees need water to grow and to stay alive. Oranges are mostly water, but they also contain valuable fiber.

WATER, WATER, EVERYWHERE

Many things dissolve easily in water. This means that drinking water usually contains minerals and other things dissolved in it. Water can also contain bacteria and poisons that harm your body. Only drink water that you know is clean and safe.

Body Talk

If you do not like the taste of tap water, use a water filter instead of buying bottled water. A filter removes some of the chemicals dissolved in the water and can improve the taste.

Making water safe

Drinking water comes from lakes and rivers or from springs and wells in the ground. In North America and in many countries, water from the faucet is treated to make sure that it is safe. Chemicals are added to it to kill any germs and remove any pollutants before it is piped into people's homes.

Chlorine is a chemical that is added to water to make it safe to drink.

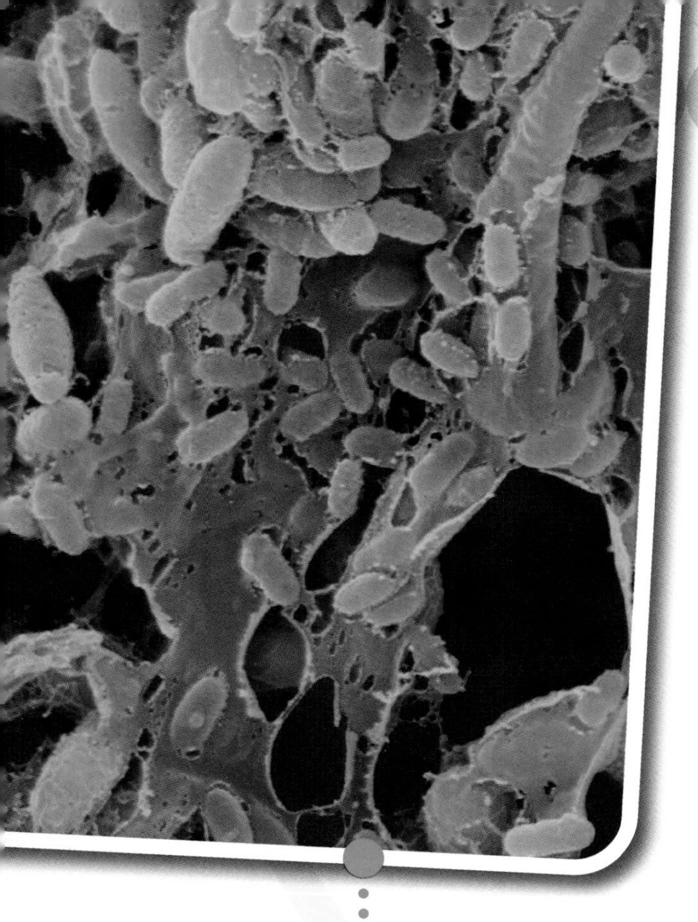

Untreated water contains harmful bacteria, which can cause diseases such as cholera.

Unreliable water

Billions of people in the world, however, do not have clean water. These countries are too poor to treat the water that people use for drinking and cooking.

Bottled water

If you are not sure the water is safe then drink only bottled water, if you can. However, plastic bottles never rot and are very bad for the environment. Only buy bottled water when there is no clean alternative.

Try this...

Collect samples of tap water, bottled water, filtered water, and ionized (alkaline) water. Dip a piece of litmus paper into each. The water in your body is pH neutral, which is between 6 and 8 pH. Which of the samples has the same value?

Did you know?

You could be drinking the same water as the dinosaurs! The same water has been circulating around Earth for billions of years. As rain flows into rivers and the sea, it evaporates and forms new rain clouds.

Other sources of water

Although plain water is very healthy, it is not the only way to drink water. All drinks consist mostly of water, and most food is more than half water, too. Although you may not realize it, you take in water every time you swallow!

Drink up!

Many drinks are made from plants. They include all fruit and vegetable juices, as well as teas made from herbs and tea leaves. Milk comes from animals and can be drunk as it is, or made into hot chocolate and other milky drinks. Sugary fruit drinks and soda pop are less healthy. They contain a lot of sugar and may have chemicals added to give them color and taste.

Try this...

Raisins are grapes that have been dried to preserve them. Soak two ounces (57 g) of raisins in half a cup (120 ml) of warm water. Leave them for an hour and then examine them. How much water is left? Where has it gone? Taste the raisins and see what has happened to them.

The juice from oranges contains a high percentage of both fiber and water.

Did you know?

About 30 percent of the total water people take in each day comes from food.

Water from food

Vegetables and fruits contain more water than other foods. A cucumber is 96 percent water! Some leafy vegetables, such as lettuce and cabbage, are more than 90 percent water. Even solid food such as chicken and tuna fish contain more than 60 percent water. Nuts, chips, and peanut butter contain the least–less than five percent water.

"I used to drink cola all the time, but now I drink water or milk. They taste just as good."

Cow's milk is made up of approximately 87 percent water.

FIBER FOODS

All plant foods contain some fiber, but some are particularly rich in it. You should try to include some foods that contain fiber in every meal.

Body Talk

Only food made from plants contains fiber. Food from animals, such as chicken, beef, fish, eggs, and dairy, contains no fiber at all.

Insoluble fiber

Peas, beans, and lentils are **legumes** that are often served as vegetables. They contain more fiber than vegetables, although all vegetables, particularly sprouts and cabbage, also contain fiber. Nuts and dried fruit, such as dates, raisins, figs, and prunes, are high in fiber, but the winner is–dried coconut.

Eat wholegrain breakfast cereals to get fiber into your daily diet.

"*Try coconut flapjacks. They load a fiber punch!*"

Wholegrain cereals

Wholegrain cereals are made from the whole grain, including the outer covering, called bran. They contain much more fiber than **refined** cereals, which have had the bran removed. Wholewheat bread has almost four times as much fiber as white bread, and brown rice has eight times as much fiber as white rice. Many breakfast cereals are high in fiber, particularly shredded wheat and bran cereals.

Rich in soluble fiber

All fruits and vegetables contain soluble fiber, but some fruits are particularly high in it. They include apples, pears, strawberries, oranges, and other citrus fruits. Peas, beans, and other legumes are also rich in soluble fiber, as are oats and barley. This makes oatmeal and other foods that contain oats good sources of soluble fiber.

Did you know?

In the past white bread was considered to be the finest bread. It was used for mass in church and eaten only by the very rich. Poorer people ate much healthier wholewheat bread!

Brown rice and broccoli are examples of foods that are high in soluble fiber.

HOW MUCH IS ENOUGH?

It is hard to say exactly how much water you need to drink every day. It varies according to how hot the weather is and how active you are. When you are short of water, your body sends out an alert–you feel thirsty!

Replacing lost water

You drink water to replace what you lose through urine, sweating, and breathing. You lose about six pints (3 l) a day, but you do not have to drink this amount of plain water. Other drinks count, and so does the water in your food. Some people advise that you should drink eight glasses of water a day, but many doctors think this is more than you actually need.

A huge amount of body fluid is lost as sweat in desert areas.

Did you know?

In very hot places, such as the Sahara Desert and Death Valley, you need to drink up to two gallons (7.5 l) of water a day!

Body Talk

Not all drinks replace lost water. Drinks that contain caffeine, such as coffee, cola, and green tea, make you urinate more and lose water. Do not count these drinks when you are counting how much water you have drunk.

"I carry a bottle of water with me to make sure I drink enough."

Extra water

You should drink extra water when you are hot and sweaty. Hot weather and exercise both make you sweat, and so does having a high temperature when you are sick. It is better to keep sipping water than to drink it all at once. If you are exercising in very hot weather, you may need to sip up to two pints (1 l) every hour.

The harder you exercise, the more you will sweat. It is important to replace lost fluids by drinking plenty of water.

You can introduce fiber into your diet by eating a healthy, high-fiber snack such as dried fruits and nuts.

How much fiber do you need?
American doctors recommend that we should eat about 0.9 to 1.3 ounces (26–38 g) of fiber a day, but most people eat much less. To eat 1.3 ounces (38 g) of fiber you would need to eat:

4 slices of wholewheat bread
1 cup (240 ml) of brown rice
½ can of baked beans
½ cup (120 ml) of lentils
1 pear
1 apple
2 oranges

See the chart on page 44 for the daily recommended amounts of fiber.

Body Talk

Children do not need as much fiber as adults because they are smaller. Children also need less fiber because they need more high-fat foods than adults to grow. If children eat too much fiber, it can fill them up and prevent them from eating high-fat foods such cheese, yogurt, and milk.

Try this...

You can get both fiber and water by making a smoothie. Chop up a banana and a mango and put them in a blender with a small cup of yogurt. Add a cup (240 ml) of fruit juice, such as apple or pineapple, and blend it together. Try different combinations of fruit to make different smoothies.

A range of foods

Fiber makes up just a small amount of any food, which means that you have to eat a range of different foods to get the fiber you need. For example, five helpings of different fruits and vegetables provides nearly half the fiber an adult needs. Snacking on nuts and dried fruit increases it further. Check the labels to find out how much fiber **processed foods** contain.

Asian diets include plenty of whole grains, seeds, and nuts, all of which are high-fiber foods.

Did you know?

Most people who live in Africa and parts of Asia eat a traditional diet that includes plenty of legumes, cereals, vegetables, and fruits. This diet is much healthier than that of many Americans.

NOT ENOUGH OR TOO MUCH?

When you do not drink enough water, your body becomes dehydrated. You may have some of the symptoms of dehydration even before you feel thirsty.

Dehydration is usually caused by not drinking enough water, but it can also be the result of losing too much water. An upset stomach that makes you vomit repeatedly or gives you diarrhea makes you lose more water. You need to drink more water than usual when you are sick.

Body Talk

When you are drinking plenty of water, your urine is almost colorless. The less water you drink, the darker the urine becomes. Urine is usually dark first thing in the morning, because you drank nothing all night. Quick–drink some water!

You need to drink about four pints (2 l) of water a day for good health. More than that can be dangerous if it is drunk too quickly.

First signs of dehydration

If you feel tired, headachy, bad-tempered, or dizzy, you are probably suffering from dehydration. As you become increasingly thirsty, your mouth, throat, and lips become dry. People who do not drink enough each day are probably slightly dehydrated all the time. When the body is short of water, the kidneys produce less urine, which means you do not pass as much urine.

Severe dehydration

When someone becomes seriously dehydrated, they get a severe headache and their eyes may look sunken. They may suffer from muscle cramps and sore joints. As their body begins to fail, they become confused, their blood pressure drops, and they lose consciousness. Their life is in grave danger, and they need emergency help.

Feeling tired and heavy is a sign of dehydration. Do not wait until you feel thirsty before you drink.

Too much water

You are not normally likely to drink too much water. When you have drank about two pints (1 l), your stomach becomes full and you do not want to drink any more. But sometimes people do drink too much, usually when they are worried about becoming dehydrated.

Urine contains minerals as well as waste products. If you drink too much water when you exercise, this can rob the body of essential nutrients.

Do not overdo it!

Some athletes are so careful not to become dehydrated, they drink too much and their kidneys cannot cope. The excess water stays in the blood, and it is then not salty enough to move in and out of the cells (see pages 32–33). This makes the cells swell, causing a condition called hyponatremia. In severe hyponatremia, water collects on the brain, which can be fatal.

Did you know?

If you drink one pint (0.45 l) of water all at once, your kidneys will filter most of it out to make extra urine. It is better to sip it slowly over an hour.

Body Talk

Athletes who might be at risk of hyponatremia from drinking too much water include competitors in endurance sports such as marathon running and long-distance cycling. Salt leaves the body when we sweat. If these athletes drink too much water, the level of sodium in their blood will fall too low.

Signs of hyponatremia

A person with hyponatremia may vomit and suffer a severe headache. They become confused and may try to drink even more water. They may suffer from cramps, seizures, or fall into a coma. Serious hyponatremia needs immediate emergency treatment.

The headache you get when you drink too much water is caused by swelling in the brain.

Body Talk

Diarrhea is caused by illness as well as by too much fiber. If the diarrhea is not too serious, you can treat it by eating less fiber. White rice, plain white bread, dry crackers, and plain yogurt are all good things to eat if you have diarrhea. Also remember to drink extra water to replace the water lost from the diarrhea.

Eating too much fiber can cause stomach pains and diarrhea. Eat a range of different foods to ensure you have a healthy digestive system.

Just enough fiber

The main problem caused by eating too little fiber is **constipation**. Everyone gets constipated occasionally, but people who do not eat enough fiber and do not drink enough water constantly suffer from constipation.

People who are frequently constipated can develop other problems when they are older. **Hemorrhoids** are small swellings just inside the **anus**. They can be extremely painful, especially when passing feces. Hemorrhoids are caused by having to strain when you use the toilet.

Too much fiber

Eating too much fiber can cause discomfort and other problems. The more fiber you eat, the faster your food moves through your **digestive system**. This can cause diarrhea. Too much fiber deprives your body of nutrients because when food moves through your body too quickly it leads to diarrhea.

Did you know?

The best way to prevent constipation is to eat plenty of fiber and drink a lot of water.

Losing nutrients

Young people should not eat too much fiber because it replaces foods with essential carbohydrates, fats, and other nutrients. Doctors say that if young children eat only wholegrain foods, they may become undernourished. For example, children should not eat a lot of raw bran. In addition, fiber can stop the body from absorbing iron, calcium, and other essential minerals.

Eating fresh fruits such as figs gives your body plenty of fiber, as well as important nutrients such as vitamins and minerals.

IT'S ON THE LABEL

Many of the foods you eat are a mixture of ingredients, each of which may contain a mixture of nutrients. Food labels include a list of ingredients and a chart of nutritional information. It tells you exactly what you are eating, including the amount of fiber.

Body Talk

Eating fiber and drinking water will help you to lose excess weight. Fiber and water fill you up so that you eat less. Fiber also absorbs some fat, so that it does not get stored in your body.

Ingredients

The ingredients are listed according to how much they contribute to the finished food. The largest ingredient is shown first and the smallest ones last. Look to see whether foods that are high in fiber are near the beginning of the list.

Nutrition Facts

Serving Size 1/4 Cup (30g)
Servings Per Container About 38

Amount Per Serving	
Calories 200 Calories from Fat 150	
	% Daily Value*
Total Fat 17g	**26%**
Saturated Fat 2.5g	**13%**
Trans Fat 0g	
Cholesterol 0mg	**0%**
Sodium 120mg	**5%**
Total Carbohydrate 7g	**2%**
Dietary Fiber 2g	**8%**
Sugars 1g	
Protein 5g	

Vitamin A 0% • Vitamin C 0%
Calcium 4% • Iron 8%

*Percent Daily Values are based on a 2,000 calorie diet.

It is important to read the labels on food packaging so you know how much fiber and nutrients the food contains.

Foods high in fiber

Most of the food groups in the food pyramid contain foods that are high in fiber. But remember that foods that come from animals, such as meat, fish, eggs, and dairy, have no fiber. Here is a useful guide to use when you shop for food:

- Nutritionists advise that half of the cereal grains you eat should be whole grain.
- All vegetables contain insoluble and soluble fiber, but peas and beans are particularly high in fiber.
- All fruit, including fruit juice, has insoluble and soluble fiber.
- In the meat and beans group, only beans and nuts contain fiber.

Did you know?

Foods are high in fiber if they contribute more than 20 percent of what you need each day. If they contribute less than five percent, they are low in fiber.

You can play an active part in the foods you eat. Visit the grocery store with your parents. Ask them to buy a range of foods that include high-fiber fruits, vegetables, and cereal products such as bread.

Healthy or unhealthy?

The foods shown in the food groups in the food pyramid on page 5 are all healthy foods. Unhealthy foods contain too much fat, salt, or sugar. The food label gives you all the information you need to decide whether a food is healthy or unhealthy.

Servings

The first thing to look at is the **serving** size. This tells you how much you are expected to eat at a time. It also shows how many servings the package contains.

Many people find that they lose weight when they cut out fatty foods and sugar and choose a high-fiber alternative instead.

Body Talk

Very often when people diet to lose weight, they cut out sugary and fatty foods. Such low-calorie diets can lead to low blood sugar. To correct this, the body sends out a signal that it needs a quick energy boost—usually as a craving for sugar. The best way to satisfy this craving healthily is to eat fiber, especially fruit.

The nutritional information provided on food labels shows the nutrients in one portion of food. If you eat two potatoes, for instance, you are consuming double the nutrients shown on the food label.

Did you know?

Some drinks are unhealthy. Soft drinks such as cola contain huge amounts of sugar, which rots your teeth.

Daily values

The nutritional information shows the amount of different nutrients in each serving. It gives the weight in grams of fat, sodium (salt), carbohydrate, dietary fiber, protein, and some vitamins and minerals. It also shows the amount of each as a percentage of the total amount you should be eating each day–the recommended Daily Values.

What to do

About one-third of your diet should be carbohydrates, but choose foods in which the carbohydrates are high in fiber. The foods to limit are those that are high in sodium, sugar, and fats. Fats to particularly look out for are saturated fats, trans fats, and cholesterol, all of which are very bad for your heart.

WATER BALANCE

Your body loses water all the time, mostly as urine, but also as sweat and in the air you breathe out. You lose as much as six pints (3 l) of water each day, which must be replaced by water you take in.

Losing water

Your kidneys produce urine to get rid of excess water and salt (see pages 34–35). However, you lose almost as much water through your skin. You perspire or sweat all the time. This helps to keep your body at a steady temperature. You sweat much more when you are hot, and if your temperature rises when you are sick. You also lose water in your feces.

"My socks smell really bad after I have exercised. I guess it is the sweat!"

Using a deodorant masks the smell of sweat and helps keep you feeling fresh.

Did you know?

Sweat contains salt. Stale sweat smells because bacteria feed on the salts and produce waste that smells bad. Washing regularly helps to keep you smelling sweet.

Breathing out

The air you breathe out contains water vapor. You can easily check this by breathing onto a mirror. The mist that forms on the cold glass consists of tiny water droplets that have condensed from the air you breathed out.

Body Talk

You lose about six pints (3 l) of water every day. This is made up of:

Water in urine
three pints (1.5 l)
Water from your skin (sweat)
two pints (0.95 l)
Water vapor from your lungs
0.9 pint (0.42 l)
Water in feces
0.44 pint (0.2 l)

On a cold day you can see the water you lose in your breath as a mist of water vapor.

Replacing lost water

You drink to replace the water you lose each day through sweat, urine, and so on. The water you drink is needed to keep every part of your body working.

Watery journey

When you drink, water and other liquids that contain water flow into your stomach. Water does not stay in the stomach for long, but quickly passes into the small **intestine**. Water does not need to be digested and soon begins to pass through the intestine wall into the blood. Minerals and vitamins B and C dissolve in water and pass along with it into the blood. Water that is carried to the large intestine along with waste is also absorbed into the blood.

Body Talk

Drinking plenty of water helps to improve your skin by keeping it moist. It also helps your kidneys to work better and the large intestine to get rid of feces.

This microscopic image shows the cells that filter blood in the kidneys. The cells remove waste products from the blood in the form of urine.

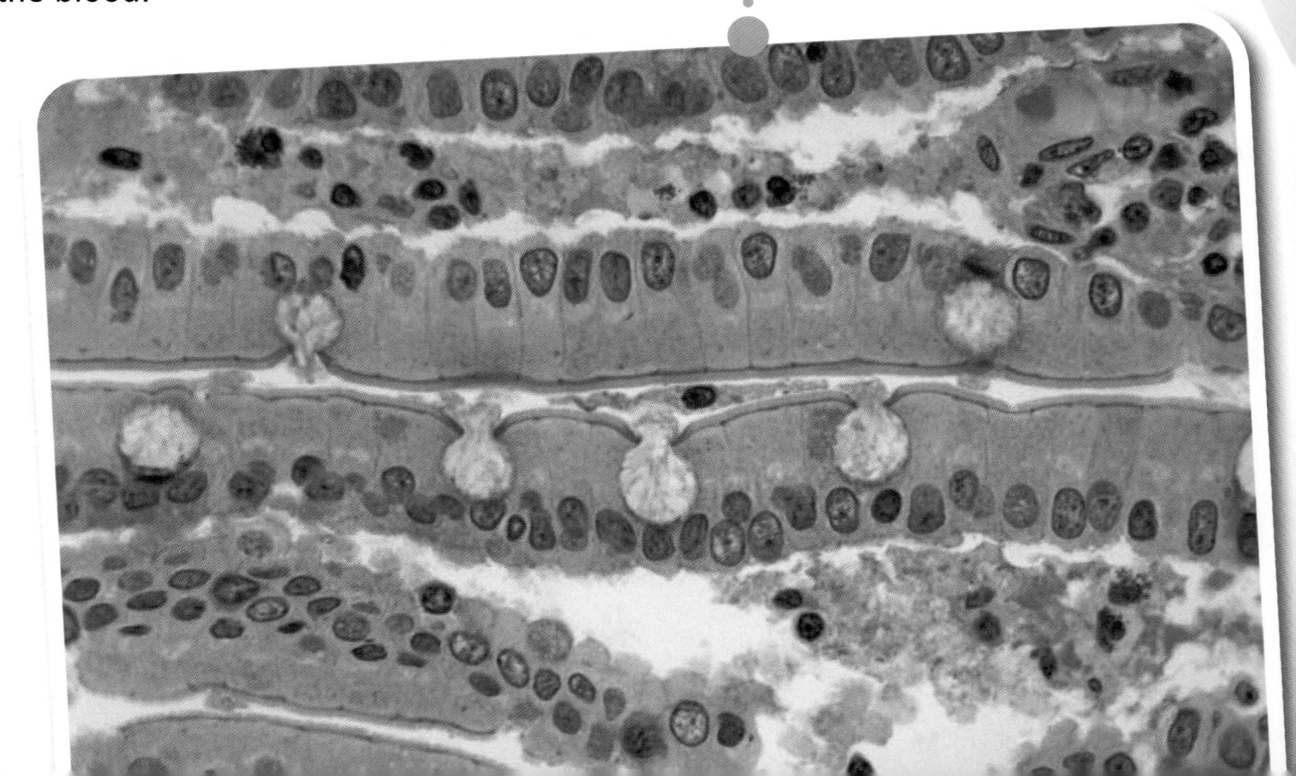

Make sure you take a drink with you when you are out and about so that you do not get dehydrated.

Did you know?

In medieval times, many people did not have access to clean drinking water, particularly in towns and cities. Instead people, including children, drank alcoholic drinks such as ale and mead. The alcohol killed the germs in the water. Today, however, we know that drinking alcohol can be very damaging to people's health.

Water in the cells

Salty water moves between the blood and the cells. It carries nutrients from foods, and oxygen from the air, into the cells. It also carries carbon dioxide waste and waste proteins out of the cells and into the blood. Water is important inside the cell, too. Many of the chemical reactions that occur in the cell involve water, such as the reaction that allows red blood cells to take carbon dioxide from the body's tissues to the lungs.

The kidneys

The kidneys control the amount of water in your blood. You have two kidneys, situated just above the back of your waist. They clean the blood by filtering out waste such as urea. This mixes with water to make urine.

Filtering system

As your cells work they produce waste proteins. The liver changes these proteins into urea, which is taken in the blood and eventually reaches the kidneys. The kidneys contain about two million tiny filters, which process about 500 gallons (1,900 liters) of blood every day. They filter out urea and other waste substances, along with excess water, to produce urine.

Body Talk

The kidneys make sure that there is enough water in the blood to balance the amount of salt in the blood. If you eat salty foods or snacks, you can help your kidneys by drinking extra water to balance the extra salt. However, regularly eating a lot of salty food, or adding a lot of salt to food, can lead to high blood pressure, which may damage the kidneys.

Camels are suited for life in hot deserts, where there is very little water. These hardy animals survive on a store of fat, seen as a hump on the camel's back.

Did you know?

Camels can survive without drinking water for months. Their urine is so concentrated it consists of solid crystals. Ouch!

Stretchy bladder

Urine trickles down two tubes, one from each kidney, to the bladder. As the bladder fills up, it stretches. It can hold up to a pint (0.45 liter), but you usually feel the need to pee when it contains about half that amount. The more you drink, the more often you have to pee.

"Eating salty food always makes me really thirsty."

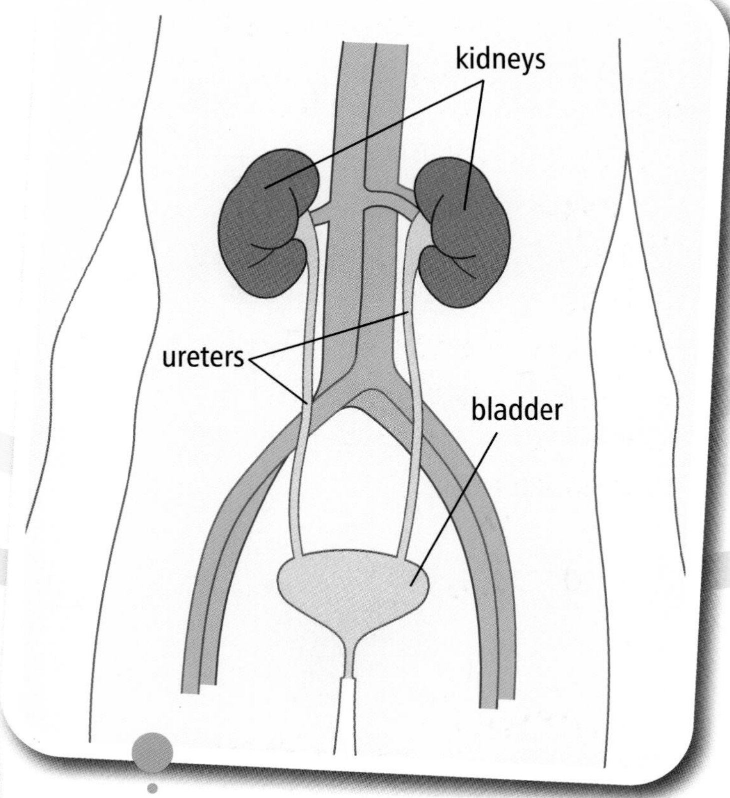

The kidneys drain urine into the bladder through long tubes called ureters. When your bladder is full it is time to visit the washroom!

WHAT CAN FIBER DO FOR YOU?

Insoluble and soluble fibers help your body in quite different ways. Insoluble fiber helps to move food through your digestive system, particularly through the large intestine (see pages 38–41). Insoluble fiber takes longer to digest, and so helps to slow down the rate at which energy is released into the body.

Soluble fiber helps to keep your heart healthy and helps to control the amount of sugar in your blood. It reduces cholesterol—a fatty substance that clogs up your heart's **arteries** and can lead to a stroke or heart attack when you are older.

Body Talk

A lifetime of eating fatty foods, such as burgers, cakes, and chocolates, and not exercising can lead to a life-threatening event such as a heart attack. Doctors recommend lifestyle changes to their patients who have suffered heart attacks. These changes include switching to a healthier diet and losing excess weight, increasing exercise, and quitting smoking.

A burger may taste good, but the fat in fast foods can cause health problems.

Help your heart by making yourself a fruit salad. Be sure to include a pear, an apple, a mandarin orange, and some strawberries.

Cholesterol

You need some cholesterol but not too much. Cholesterol builds up slowly. The damaging effects are not usually felt until you are middle aged. Nevertheless, the process can begin when you are young. Soluble fiber contains pectin and gum, which bind up cholesterol and keep it from sticking to the walls of your arteries.

Fresh fruits are excellent sources of insoluble fiber and essential nutrients such as carbohydrates, vitamins, and minerals.

"*Eating fast food makes me feel really tired. I prefer to eat healthier foods and have a lot of energy.*"

DIGESTION

Food has to be digested before the body can use the nutrients in it. The digestive system breaks the food up so that the nutrients can pass into your blood. Although water and fiber are not digested, they help the digestive system work.

Breaking down food

When you swallow, food passes down a tube into the stomach and then into a long, thin tube called the small intestine. Here, digestive juices break up the food into smaller and smaller **molecules**, until they are so small they slip through the thin wall of the small intestine into the blood. Water with minerals and some vitamins dissolved in it also passes into the blood.

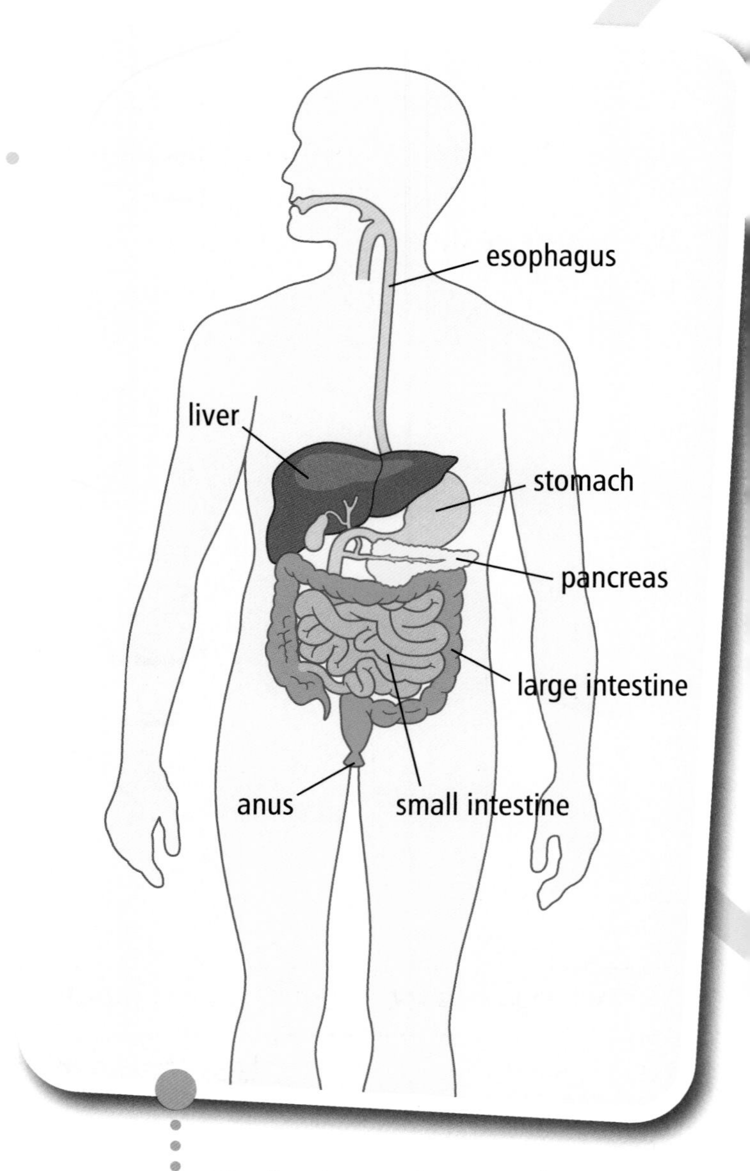

The food we eat passes down a tube called the ***esophagus*** *into the stomach. The partially digested food then moves to the small intestine. The walls of the small intestine absorb most of the nutrients in our food. The waste then passes through the large intestine and out through the anus.*

Helpful fiber

A thick, soupy mixture of undigested food, digestive juices, and dead cells then passes into a wider tube called the large intestine or bowel. Food moves through the digestive system because the sides of the tube squeeze it forward, like you squeeze a tube of toothpaste. If the waste in the large intestine contains a lot of bulky fiber, it is easier for the tube to push it forward.

As the waste passes through the large intestine, water continues to move into the blood, so that the waste, now called feces, becomes more solid. Feces leave the body through the anus.

Body Talk

Food with a lot of fiber in it can help you lose weight. The fiber fills you up and takes longer to digest, which means you eat less.

Did you know?

It takes one to two days for fiber to pass through the digestive system.

How long does food take to pass through the body?	
In the mouth	Less than a minute
In the stomach	Up to four hours
In the small intestine	About seven hours
In the large intestine	Up to about 20 hours

The long, stringy parts of celery are fibrous and help to sweep waste foods from the intestine.

Body Talk

Some foods, including some high-fiber foods, increase the amount of gas made in the large intestine. Bacteria that help to break down undigested foods, including fiber, produce the gas. The gas is expelled from the anus.

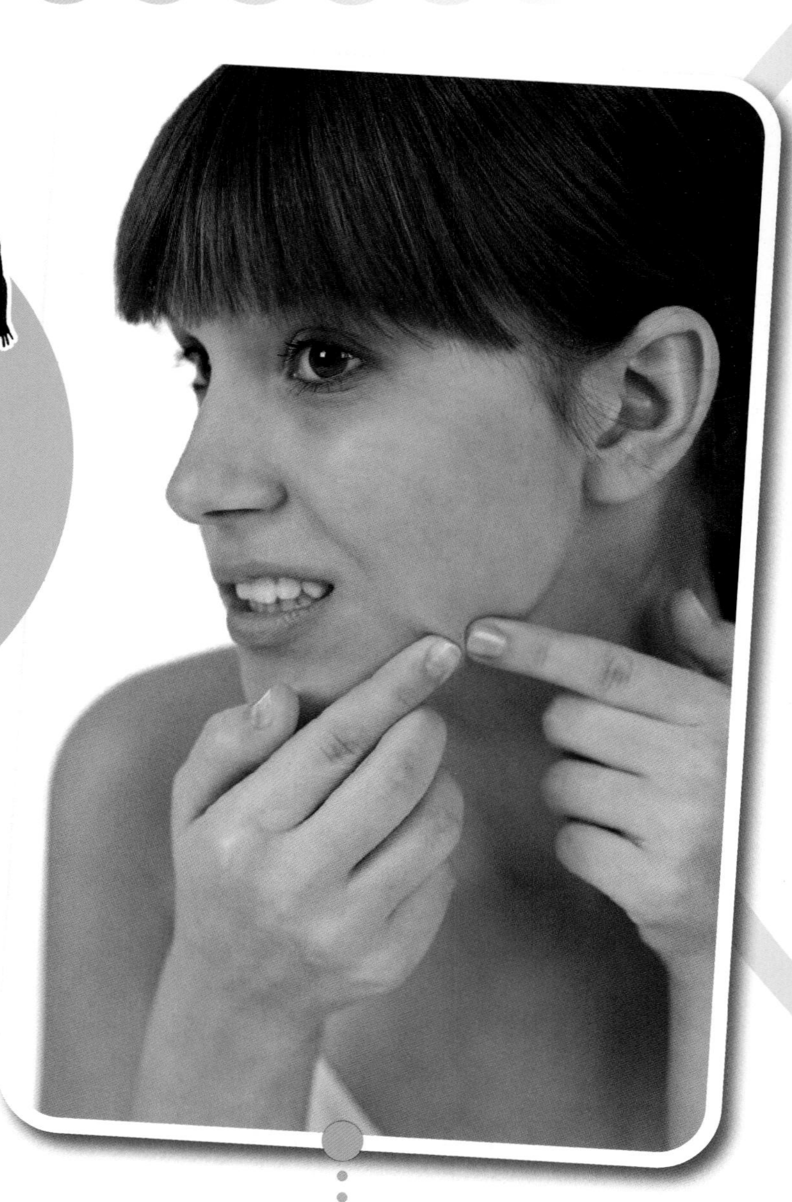

Frequent constipation is one possible cause of acne. You can avoid this by eating high-fiber foods and drinking a lot of water.

Not too fast or too slow

The amount of fiber and water in your diet helps to control how fast feces move through the large intestine. Too much fiber or a stomach bug can cause diarrhea, while too little fiber causes constipation.

Too fast

If feces move through your large intestine too quickly, there is not enough time for water to pass through the wall of the bowel into the blood. This means the feces contain more water, so you are more likely to suffer from diarrhea.

Too slow

When your food contains too little fiber, less undigested food passes into the bowel (the large intestine). The feces then move more slowly through the bowel and become more solid, as more water passes out of the bowel into the blood. The feces become dry and hard and are difficult to push out of the body. This is called constipation.

Bad diets and health problems

People who eat a bad diet with too much red meat and not enough fiber are more likely to get **colon** cancer. The cancer grows on the wall of the bowel and has to be cut out. If it is not treated quickly, the cancer may spread to other parts of the body.

Did you know?

It does not matter how often you use the toilet–once a day, more or less often–as long as, when you do go, the feces are soft but not runny.

Pears are a tasty snack and healthy, too. These fruits are rich in soluble and insoluble fiber.

FOOD ALLERGIES AND SPECIAL DIETS

If you are advised to eat a healthier diet, either to lose weight or to help your digestive system to work better, it is likely to include more fiber and more water. Some people are allergic to particular forms of fiber, however, and always have to be careful which foods they choose.

If you decide to increase the amount of fiber in your diet, do so gradually. Your digestive system needs to adjust to the new foods. Do not increase your intake of fiber by more than a few ounces every few days. Make sure you drink plenty of water at the same time.

Body Talk

Here are some easy ways to increase the amount of fiber in your diet:

Eat shredded wheat or muesli for breakfast.
Make sandwiches with wholewheat bread.
Choose snacks such as nuts and dried fruits.
EAT PLENTY OF FRUITS AND VEGETABLES!

Pizza is a popular food, but people with celiac disease cannot eat it because they are allergic to gluten in the pizza dough.

Allergy to gluten

Gluten is a protein that is found in many cereal grains. Wheat is particularly high in gluten, and gluten is often added to bread to make it bouncier. People with celiac disease are allergic to gluten. They have to avoid eating anything that contains wheat and other cereals, apart from barley and rye.

Allergy to water

A few people are allergic to, or react badly to, some of the chemicals dissolved in water from the faucet. They have to drink filtered water or bottled water instead.

Try this...

Design a day's healthy diet for someone with celiac disease. Remember that no wheat means no bread (except rye bread), no pasta, and no pizza.

Drinking water is the best way to stay hydrated. Try bottled or filtered water if you do not like the taste of faucet water.

FOOD FACTS AND STATS

Daily recommended amount of fiber

Age in years	Weight
1–3	0.67 oz (19 g)
4–8	0.88 oz (25 g)
Males 9–13	1.09 oz (31 g)
14–18	1.34 oz (38 g)
19–50	1.34 oz (38 g)
Over 50	1.06 oz (30 g)
Females 9–18	0.9 oz (26 g)
19–50	0.88 oz (25 g)
Over 50	0.74 oz (21 g)

Another way to calculate the amount of fiber is to allow 0.5 ounces (14 g) for every 1,000 calories of your diet. If a man eats 2,500 calories a day, he should be getting 1.25 ounces (35 g) of fiber. If a woman eats 2,000 calories, she should be getting one ounce (28 g) of fiber. These amounts vary slightly from those in the table above.

Daily recommended amount of water

Six to eight glasses, but more when sweating due to weather, exercise, or fever.

Amount of fiber in selected foods

Food	Serving	Weight of fiber	Percentage by weight
Wholewheat bread	1 slice	0.06 oz (1.7 g)	5.8%
White bread	1 slice	0.02 oz (0.6 g)	1.5%
Brown rice	1 cup (240 ml)	0.12 oz (3.4 g)	0.8%
White rice	1 cup (240 ml)	0.02 oz (0.6 g)	0.1%
Shredded wheat	2 squares	0.19 oz (5.4 g)	11.6%
Porridge	1 cup (240 ml)	0.14 oz (4.0 g)	6.1%
Cornflakes	1 cup (240 ml)	0.02 oz (0.6 g)	0.9%
Baked beans (canned)	1 cup (240 ml)	0.37 oz (10.4 g)	3.7%
Lentils (cooked)	1 cup (240 ml)	0.55 oz (15.6 g)	1.9%
Peas	1 cup (240 ml)	0.16 oz (4.5 g)	5.1%
Sweet corn	1 cup (240 ml)	0.14 oz (4.0 g)	1.4%
Beetroot	1 cup (240 ml)	0.1 oz (2.9 g)	1.9%
Peanuts	1 oz (28 g)	0.08 oz (2.3 g)	6.0%
Almonds	1 oz (28 g)	0.12 oz (3.4 g)	7.4%
Raisins	1 cup (240 ml)	0.19 oz (5.4 g)	5.3%
Dried coconut	1 oz (28 g)	0.14 oz (4.0 g)	13.7%
Banana	1 fruit	0.11 oz (3.1 g)	1.1%
Apple	1 fruit	0.12 oz (3.4 g)	1.5%
Pear	1 fruit	0.18 oz (5.1 g)	2.2%
Orange	1 fruit	0.11 oz (3.1 g)	1.7%

Percentage of water in selected foods

Food	Percentage by weight	Food	Percentage by weight
Cucumber	96%	Peach	90%
Lettuce	95%	Orange	86%
Mushrooms	93%	Wholewheat bread	38%
Peas	78%	Spaghetti	74%
Potatoes	80%	Brown rice	66%
Apple	85%	Cheddar cheese	36%
Banana	75%	Tuna fish	75%

GLOSSARY

anus The end of the digestive tract through which feces is expelled from the body

arteries Blood vessels that carry blood away from the heart to the rest of the body

cell Tiny structure that makes up the bodies of all living things; cells group together to form tissues which, in turn, group to form organs

cellulose Carbohydrate that makes up the cell wall of plants

colon Lower part of the bowels, where food is changed into waste

constipation When feces are too dry and hard and are difficult to push out of the body

dehydrated Lacking water

digestive system Part of the body that turns food into elements your body needs

esophagus Muscular tube that runs from your throat to your stomach

feces Solid waste matter that passes out of the anus

germ Microscopic organism that harms the body, causing disease

hemorrhoid Small, swollen blood vessel just inside the anus

insoluble fiber Type of fiber that passes through the body without being absorbed

intestine Long tube in the body through which food passes after leaving the stomach

legume Pod, such as a pea or bean

molecule Smallest part of a substance

nutrient Healthy source of nourishment

pectin Chemical substance found in some fruits that helps keep your heart healthy

processed food Food which has been prepared in a factory using several ingredients and other substances such as salt and chemicals

refined Made fine or pure by an industrial process

saliva Watery mixture in the mouth

serving Portion of food

soluble fiber Portion of food that is not absorbed by the body but is soluble in water

urine Liquid waste from the body (pee)

FURTHER READING

Keep a weekly food diary and write down the fibrous foods that you eat during the week. Do you think you eat enough fiber?

Books

Sayer, Dr. Melissa, *Too Fat? Too Thin? The Healthy Eating Guidebook*. Crabtree Publishing, 2009.

Doeden, Matt, *Eat Right*, Lerner, 2009.

Gardner, Robert, *Health Science Projects about Nutrition*. Enslow Publishers, 2002.

Royston, Angela. *Water and Fiber for a Healthy Body*. Heinemann-Raintree, 2009.

Sohn, Emily, and Sarah Webb. *Food and Nutrition*. Chelsea Clubhouse, 2006.

Internet

Harvard School of Public Health
www.hsph.harvard.edu/nutritionsource/healthy-drinks/
www.hsph.harvard.edu/nutritionsource/what-should-you-eat/fiber/index.html

Your Digestive System
http://kidshealth.org/kid/htbw/digestive_system.html

Your Gross and Cool Body
http://yucky.discovery.com/flash/body/pg000126.html

INDEX